Ready, Steady, Go, Cheetah!

Pat Moon

Illustrated by Woody

ORCHARD BOOKS

Chimp was very cross.
Someone had stuck something to
his favourite tree.
"Oi! Who's been messing up my
tree?" he shouted.
"Keep the noise down," yawned
Cheetah from his branch.

"Wait a minute," said Elephant.
"It's got words on it. Can anyone
here read?"

6

Turtle was just back from his swim.

He read it out:

"Come and join the fun at the Lakeside Sports."

"Sports?" yelled Cheetah. "Yeah! Read on, Turtle."

Turtle read on: "Three legged race..."

"Did you say three legs?" asked Chimp.

Turtle nodded.

"No good for me, then," moaned Chimp. "I've only got two legs.

"I don't have enough legs for that one," said Chimp.

"Never heard of anyone with three legs," said Elephant.

"Three legs?" said Cheetah. "Dead easy! I could beat anyone – just using three legs. Or two legs. One leg even!"

"What else is there?" asked Crane.

"R u n n i n g race," said Turtle.

"Yeah!" cried C h e e t a h. "F a s t e s t thing on four legs, too! Wham! Zap! Zoom!"

"There's high jump," said Turtle.
"No problem!" yelled Cheetah,
leaping over a branch.

Elephant took a run at the branch
...and leapt!

CRASH! Down she fell.
The ground shook.
A coconut landed on her head.

"Maybe I won't bother with the high jump," said Elephant.
"What about the obstacle race?" asked Turtle.

"It's when there are things in the way and you have to go under or over or through them," explained Turtle.

"I'm good at over and under!"
cried Chimp.
"But not as fast as me," boasted
Cheetah.
To show how fast he was, he
leapt over Chimp

and slithered under Elephant.

"How about you, Turtle? Are you going to the Sports?" asked Crane.

"Yep!" said Turtle. "But not this one. I'm going to a better one than that. Now, can't stop. Lots to do."

Turtle had an idea.

Later, a different poster was stuck to Chimp's tree.

Chimp, quick!

"Someone's messed up your tree again!" shrieked Crane.
"It's OK," said Chimp. "Turtle put it there. See those words? They say: Use of tree by kind permission of CHIMP."

"What else does it say?" asked Crane.

No one knew until Turtle read it to them.

Come and Join in
Turtle's Sports Day.
FUN
something for everyone!
something for:
elephants
chimps &
cranes.
Prizes for winners!
Next saturday.
(use of tree by kind permission
of chimp.)

"What about us cheetahs?" asked
Cheetah.

"You'll be at the Lakeside
Sports," said Turtle.
"It's on the same day. You can't
do both."

"What?" cried Cheetah. "No one's coming to see me win all those prizes? Well – I'll have to do this one instead.
Don't want you to miss me."

So Turtle added:

"Now, Elephant," said Turtle, "your big feet are just what we need to tread a race track."

"Chimp – we'll need sticks and ropes for starting and finishing lines."

"Crane – can you sort out some prizes?"

Ah, perfect! Wait till I get to work on these!

"And Cheetah – you get everyone fit."

On Saturday morning everything was ready.

Race one, is the LOG RACE.

"First one to reach the big log…"
"*Too* easy," grinned Cheetah.
"…has to carry it to the finishing line," said Turtle.
"What?" said Cheetah.

They were off!
Cheetah was there first. But he couldn't budge the log.
Nor could Chimp.
Or Crane.

But Elephant just curled her trunk round that log and lifted it like it weighed nothing at all! Then off she jogged.

"Elephant's the winner!" cried Turtle.

"I could've lifted that – if Elephant hadn't just barged in," said Cheetah.

"Race two is the BANANA RACE," called Turtle.
"First one back with a banana is the winner."

They were off!

Cheetah was first down the track – and into the jungle – with Crane flying close behind and Elephant chasing them.

But suddenly Chimp was there!
Climbing up, swinging down and
racing back – with a banana!

"Chimp's the winner!" cried
Turtle.

"I could've won easily," said Cheetah, "if it wasn't for those stupid trees."

"Race three is the OBSTACLE RACE," called Turtle.

Where's the obstacle?

There!

"First one to reach the other side of the river is the winner," said Turtle.
"READY, STEADY, GO!"

Cheetah was splashing through.
Elephant was wading under, with Chimp clinging to her trunk.
"Help!" cried Chimp.
"Just you hang on tight, Chimp," said Elephant.

Then suddenly Crane took off, flying over the river to the other side!

"Crane's the winner!" called Turtle as he swam.

"Race four is the RUNNING
RACE," called Turtle.
"First one round the lake to the
crooked tree on the other side - is
the winner."

They were off!
Elephant was charging on.
Chimp was scooting along.
Crane was flapping and striding out, but Cheetah was a *flash* as he *streaked* ahead!

Then he was just a cloud of dust!

"What do you say about teaching
Cheetah a lesson?" asked Turtle.
"Good idea!" they all agreed.
"Listen…" said Turtle. "This is
what we do…"

Quickly, Turtle led them along a
path to the crooked tree, which
was near the Lakeside Sports.

And while they waited for Cheetah, Elephant fetched cups of jungle juice from the refreshment stall.

Then they saw Cheetah pounding towards them.

"Ready everyone?" said Turtle.

"Ready!" they said.

Cheetah could not believe his
eyes.
"This can't be real!" he cried.
"How come you all beat me?"
"No problem!" boasted Elephant.
"Dead easy," said Chimp.

Cheetah flopped to the ground.
"You mean no prize?" he asked
sadly.
"No three cheers? Nothing?"

And they began to feel quite sorry for Cheetah.
Chimp leapt up and put his arm round him.

"It was only a joke, Cheetah! We tricked you!"
"We took a short cut," said Elephant.
"Got tired of your boasting," said Crane.

"YOU are the fastest thing on four legs!" said Turtle.

"Do I get three cheers?" asked Cheetah quietly.

"Three cheers for Cheetah!" yelled Turtle.

HIP, HIP, HOORAY!

And they rewarded him with a double jungle juice.

When they got back, Crane gave out the prizes.
First to Elephant.
"What is it?" asked Elephant.
"It's a sun-hat," said Crane.

why - so it is - just what I need!

Then to Chimp.
"What is it?" asked Chimp.
"It's a banana holder," said Crane.

I've always wanted a banana holder!

Then to Cheetah.
"What is it?" asked Cheetah.
"It's a sunshade," said Crane.
"See?"

"And this is for me," said Crane.
"What is it?" everyone asked.
"It's a shopping bag."

Then to Turtle.

"For organising everything," said Crane.

"What is it?" asked Turtle.

"It's a turtle hammock," said Crane.

"Everyone's a winner!" cried Elephant. "Three cheers for Turtle!

HIP, HIP, HOORAY!"